To Jack,
S.McB.

For Deirdre,
A.J.

First published 2007 by Walker Books Ltd
87 Vauxhall Walk, London SE11 5HJ

10 9 8 7 6 5 4 3 2 1

Text © 2007 Sam McBratney
Illustrations © 2007 Anita Jeram

Guess How Much I Love You™ is a registered
trademark of Walker Books Ltd, London

The right of Sam McBratney and Anita Jeram to be
identified as author and illustrator respectively of this
work has been asserted by them in accordance with
the Copyright, Designs and Patents Act 1988

This book has been typeset in Cochin

Printed and bound in China

British Library Cataloguing in
Publication Data: a catalogue record
for this book is available from the
British Library

ISBN 978-1-4063-0854-9

www.walkerbooks.co.uk

GUESS HOW MUCH
I LOVE YOU
—— in the ——
SUMMER

Written by
Sam McBratney

Illustrated by
Anita Jeram

WALKER BOOKS
AND SUBSIDIARIES
LONDON · BOSTON · SYDNEY · AUCKLAND

Little Nutbrown Hare
and Big Nutbrown Hare were down
by the river on a summer's day.

On a summer's day there
are colours everywhere.

"Which blue do you like best?"
asked Little Nutbrown Hare.

Big Nutbrown Hare didn't know –
there were so many lovely blues.

"I think ... maybe the sky,"
he said.

Big Nutbrown Hare
looked across the river.
There were grasses and ferns
and tall plants swaying
in the breeze.

"Which green do you
like best?" he asked.

Little Nutbrown Hare began to think,
but he didn't really know.
So many lovely things
were green.

"Maybe the big leaves," he said.

Now it was
Little Nutbrown
Hare's turn to
pick a colour.

He spotted a ladybird, and some poppies.

"What's your favourite
red?" he asked.

Big Nutbrown Hare
thought about red things,
but it was hard to choose
just one.

"I think those
berries," he said.

Big Nutbrown Hare nibbled
a dandelion leaf.

"Which yellow do you
like best?"

There were so many yellows!
Little Nutbrown Hare even
saw some yellows
buzzing about.
How could he
possibly choose?

"Maybe these flowers,"
he said.

Then Little Nutbrown Hare began
to smile and smile.

He looked at Big Nutbrown Hare and said,

"Which brown do you like best?"

And Big Nutbrown Hare smiled too.
There were many many lovely browns,
but one was the best of all...

"Nutbrown!"